LIGHTNING STRIKER

MALIK ABDUS-SABR JR

To order additional copies of this book, contact:
Xlibris
844-714-8691
www.Xlibris.com
Orders@Xlibris.com

ISBN: Softcover   978-1-6641-7320-0
        EBook   978-1-6641-7319-4

Print information available on the last page

Rev. date: 05/04/2021

Acknowledgements

I would like to give a special thanks to everyone who was involved in this book writing process alongside me. This book is dedicated to my Grandfather Anthony Parker. For always allowing me to share my superhero ideas with him starting back in 2016. I want to thank my friends Hunter and Ted for bringing back my love for superheroes back in my sophomore year of high school when Captain America Civil War came to theaters.

For my readers, with this being my first published work, it warms my heart knowing you all would take time out of your day and read my work. I am truly grateful, and I hope you all stay up on my future projects.

All my love and blessings,
Malik Abdus-Sabr JR

Preface

Lightning Striker has been a superhero story I've been writing and rewriting since I was in the third grade. How he came to be was peculiar in its own way but I still made it work. In third grade, I had a crush on a girl, a kitty love but my first love. She was always smart, reading Harry Potter books during Friday recess. One day I asked her why she liked Harry Potter so much. She stated "he's the closest thing to a hero in my eyes."

That day when I got home, it was a stormy afternoon so my mother told me I couldn't play outside. I was very creative in my elementary school years with drawing. I always loved to draw, starting out with drawing Pokemon and Yugioh. However, at that moment, I needed to draw something else. I needed to draw a hero for my crush. In my mom's room where she kept her computer paper, I grabbed a couple and got to drawing.

I drew two heroes. First guy would be the main hero while the other is the sidekick. The first hero was a guy who's costume had all the colors on it. I called him "Rainbow Shiner." Only reason why I didn't take the first hero seriously was because I drew his body in the way that looked like a triangle, and it turned me off from him being my main hero. The second hero I drew was supposed to be the sidekick, this time I was extra careful in drawing him and used my favorite colors. The same colors for the home uniform of the old NFL team, the Houston Oilers. The powder blue, white, and red made this hero look more appealing to my eye.

I presented my hero to my crush, and it made her smile from ear to ear. I guess this is where I started to slowly put drawing to the side and work more on creative writing. Mainly because often time in class I would daydream about my hero, Lightning Striker. And around this time, now one of my favorite movies of all time had come to theaters. X-men Origins: Wolverine (2009). This was around the same time WATCHMEN (2009) had come to theaters also. Those two gritty movies showed me from a young age the true meanings of real life, or the closest to it. And I am grateful that I didn't fall into the fallacy of the hero life in the cinema world. However, Spider-Man 2 (2004), TMNT (2007), and Teen Titans (2003-2006) have played significant roles in my superhero creation.

From then on I started writing more about his backstory. I chose Hawaii because of the first book I read after that idea came into my head. It was called *Magic Treehouse: High Tide In Hawaii*. The small aspects of Hawaiian culture that was shown in the book intrigued my nine year old brain for some odd reason. And as this book is being completed, I still haven't been. That's where I chose where he was from. His appearance is based off of a WWE wrestler who looked up to par with being a superhero, *Rey Mysterio.* His mask and clothing attire is beloved among many wrestling fans, me choosing to implement that in with my own variation is a prime example of Rey Mysterio's fanbase. Lightning Striker's powers are based on the powers I imagined myself having back then if I truly were a hero.

Looking back, I started this journey when I was only eight years old. Now being twenty-one, I don't feel like this is a weight lifted off of my shoulders. I feel more anxious than relieved, but it's a good kind of anxious feeling. I truly know and believe that ten years down from now I'll be sitting alongside the giants of the comic book world while being one of them. All stories have to start somewhere, my superhero story started in spring 2009. Now, twelve years later, my dreams are coming to fruition. With this only being my third published book, I have a ways to go, but trust and believe I will get there. Welcome to the beginning of Sau Titan, AKA Lightning Striker.

Prologue

This story takes place solely on the islands of Hawaii with the capital city Honolulu being a focus. The late summer of 2007 leading to through the early fall ties into some true events that happened with the world at the time, with a few creative spins on them.

The other heroes and villains featured in this story have backgrounds that will be expressed in other stories of mine. The order of which my comic books are distributed are in chronological order, however, there are many storylines I've created related to Lightning Striker that happen before his birth. Dating back to even the attacks on Pearl Harbor that I tie in, those storylines that I publish in the future will be the prequels.

Certain dates, names and areas I stated about Honolulu in the book are fictional and were used for creative purposes.

LIGHTNING STRIKER

BIRTH OF THE WARRIOR

Tamina struggled to get off the couch due to the size of her stomach. She had been pregnant for eight months with her second child, as her first born, Raymundo, helped her walk to the kitchen. Her husband Noel, had just come in the house from mowing the lawn, grass clippings in his unruly hair.

"Noel, I need some more of that juice, my stomach is hurting again." Tamina gestured over to the fridge. As he nodded his head and took a glass out of the cabinet, she suddenly clutched onto Raymundo's arm with a tight grip. "Uh-oh, Noel my water just broke." Tamina's voice got higher with every word that came out.

"Raymundo go and get your shoes on, we're going to the hospital." Noel smiled while now assisting his wife. "You had a five year gap between kids, it doesn't feel any easier huh?" Noel tried to make light of the situation. She looked up at him and gave him a light shake of the head. Once on the road, Tamina kept screaming in pain as Noel saw nothing but agony in her eyes.

"Noel, I can't wait any more. I'm having this baby right now!" Tamina screamed. That just made him accelerate the gas as the car sped off to the hospital.

Raymundo looked over from the backseat and noticed his mom's blouse soaked with blood.

"Dad, Mommy has blood on her." Noel looked down and gasped.

"Here goes the hospital." Noel drove into the parking lot and they all hurried into the emergency room. Once there, it didn't take long for a team of doctors to rush in with a gurney.

"Thank you God!" Tamina blurted out. She looked at Noel and Raymundo, as they stood together looking back at her. "My boys, I love you both." She gave them a big wide smile just to reassure them that everything would be okay. The doctors carefully hauled her off while one stayed back to talk to the family.

"There was a lot of blood, we may need to do an emergency c-section. And from the laws that have passed, the father is not allowed in the room for something like that. Not until after the baby is delivered." A wave of disappointment settled in his stomach, mainly for not being there to see his new baby's first breaths of the world.

"Alright, we'll wait right here until you guys are done." They exchanged a handshake before Noel took Raymundo to the waiting area.

After a few hours a doctor finally came out to talk to an exhausted Noel and Raymundo.

"Sir, it's a boy." Noel and Raymundo cheered simultaneously.

"Thank you, thank you doctor. How did my wife react? She's been hoping for a girl ever since this one right here was born." Raymundo gave a shrug still smiling. The doctor stood still, an awkward silence filling the waiting room. "I asked you a question." Noel repeated.

"Mr. Titan, as you know she started bleeding before she got here." Noel lost all the breath in his body.

"Go get my wife."

"It's not easy to say-."

"Go get my wife!"

"Your wife was having complications with the baby and-."

"GO! GET! MY! WIFE!"

"Your wife died after delivering the baby." The doctor let out. Noel closed his eyes trying to wake up. All he saw were moments filled with dates from college, their honeymoon, watching the sunrise together, their wedding. He opened his eyes to a tear filled blurry vision of the doctor.

"Daddy, is what he said about mommy true?" Raymundo grabbed onto his father's wrist.

"Yes son, it's true."

"Mr. Titan. I deeply regret informing you this. As you know complications affect the mother and the child. Your son is very sick. And I mean dangerously sick. It's a miracle he's still breathing."

"I can't lose my wife and my son. I can't do it." A defeated Noel sank to his knees in front of Raymundo. Another doctor who had been paying attention the whole time, came up and whispered something to the operating Doctor.

"Mr. Titan. There is something that may work. It hasn't passed U.S. legislation, and it's a risky-."

"Do whatever you can to make my son live. Now." He stated. The doctor nodded his head and went back into the room.

Hours later, Noel sat silently with his hands in his lap. *Why didn't I tell her I loved her?* Kept his thoughts filled with just that one question. He looked over at his oldest child sleeping soundly. For all he knows, this could be his only child.

"Sir!" The same doctor yelled from the operating room. Noel quickly shook to wake up Raymundo. After walking into the room, there he saw. His second son. Still whimpering with his eyes tightly closed. *Beautiful.* He thought as his hand rested on Raymundo's shoulder.

"What did you do?"

"Well, we injected a quarter the size of *Electorpais* in his feet and chest. The little scar looks like a birthmark." Noel walked over to the "crib" where his son lay.

"Electorpais?"

"Yes. It's a version of Plutonium. Forever energy that only gets stronger over time. Meaning your son will get stronger over time. The original Pais was altered."

"So why isn't it legal? You just saved my son."

"You know how due process works don't you? Usually that's with breaking the law. And my authority broke the law for you to have your son."

"That doesn't answer my question." The doctor hesitated. Noel looked up and saw what he thought was a male nurse practitioner. His piercing blue eyes made a brave Noel feel uncomfortable. He then carefully picked up his newborn child. Forgetting the conversation prior.

"Sau. I will name this boy Sau. Sau Titan. Warrior of Hawaii. Look Ray, it's your youngest brother." Baby Sau stopped whimpering and laid still in his father's arms. His big brown eyes looking up like he was telling Noel a message. The doctor walked back in to where the doctors were all mucking about their work. Now being able to talk to the other doctor, the one with the blue eyes.

"Big man, but he's a weak man. The desperation in his eyes proved how weak some men can be. Now tell me Sczar, why would we give a newborn baby double the dose of electorpais?" White-Cell asked his top seeker henchman.

"I say it is a mere test. Electorpais has never been used on a baby or for a medical reason. Think of it as a way to expand the seeker army. We must be innovative, that child may be the blueprint to help us level up."

"A human baby has no instincts. It has to be taught everything. That baby has a father who will teach him his ways. His weak ways. I need to teach it to work for me." White-Cell had smiled at the thought that came to his mind. "I have to kill the father."

"Give it some time White-Cell. And plan it. We've just got out of battle on the mainland, in which we lost a significant amount of seekers. Don't rush, abide your time." He now thought as he walked towards the exit of the hospital.

"Quite smart of you to think to do our operations in a hospital. Getting us access to all of Hawaii's medicines. Testing them to amplify this electorpais."

"And yet all of them have failed except the alteration you used last night. Adding the electrical component to the Pais that made us who we are, which was put into that baby just now. Worst case scenario, the baby doesn't live long."

"See that's where you're wrong. Worst case scenario is the kid realizing his powers and not being led by me. We can dominate, and put the plan in motion."

"And what is that plan White-Cell?" They both looked at each other with deep intensity.

"You'll see. But for now, I want all the information on that boy. When the time is right, I'll collect what is mine."

7 Years Later

Sau sat in the living room watching cartoons while his father was making Poi. Raymundo warming up on the punching bag a couple feet from the couch. Sau saw the cowboy on TV snap his fingers, and as he copied him, a bright little spark came off as he snapped. Interested, Sau did it again. More sparks. Leaving it alone, he turned to his father in the kitchen. Sau always admired his father, with his wild hair and big stature, he looked like the samoan rugby players they watched on TV.

"Dad, why do you like watching the sunrise with me and Ray?" A sad smile came upon his face. Before Noel could answer, there was a brief knock at the door. Turning off the stove, Noel opened the door to greet two men in suits. They spoke softly but urgently and the conversation got more tense as the seconds went by.

"So that supplement you put in my child, this is some sort of recall? I don't think so!" Raymundo and Sau paid more attention as their father became more enraged. "Raymundo, take Sau and run!" Noel pushed the two men outside and began to fight as Raymundo threw his gloves down.

"Sau, go in your room and hide." Raymundo picked up his metal baseball bat.

"That's my daddy too, I'm helping." They both ran out of the house to help Noel. All Sau could do was watch his father pummel one man as hard as he could. Raymundo kept swinging his bat at the other guy, but he kept dodging it and finally tackled him. "Help!" Sau kept yelling in panic. No one could hear them though, they lived in a small rural town on the big island. With very few neighbors in close distance. Two more men emerged from the van, not expecting a fight.

"Get this bastard off of me!" The one guy yelled as Noel kept bashing his head into the ground. The two attacked Noel, getting him onto his back and started to tie him up. The guy who was on the ground wiped the blood from his head and started walking towards Sau. Fear consumed him as he looked into those piercing blue eyes of the man in front of him. "Alas, my prize. Throw the other two in the truck." The man with the blue eyes grabbed Sau's armed and dragged him towards the van. The family kept struggling to get free but with no avail.

"Let's drive." The other man said as they hauled the family into the back.

"Speed up a little." The man with the blue eyes pulled Sau closer to him and smiled. "So tell me Sau, are you afraid of me?" Noel kicked him in the stomach before Sau could answer. Raymundo broke free of one's grasp and gouged the driver's eye. The car turned violently and came to an abrupt stop. Raymundo grabbed his little brother as Noel grabbed one man's pistol and shot him. Startled, he'd never seen a purple like laser. All three of them jumped out the back of the van and took off running. Noel looked back and saw the four men starting to chase them, they were a little bit away but slowly gained on them.

"Raymundo. We don't have much time. Take your baby brother to Oahu. Kaimana beach to be exact.

There is a fish boat from Kailua bay that goes there every night, sneak in through the back." He handed

Sau a locket. Looking back, he saw how much closer they were. He knew now that *they* weren't normal with claws like that, running hunched over like cavemen. He had to do what he thought could save both of his kids, even if he dies in the process. "Daddy loves you both. Go now to the bay and don't stop. I'm doing this to save my sons, do as I say." The kids hugged their dad one quickly before doing what they were told. Noel fired shots winging a couple. Sau looked back at the scene, watching his father toss the gun away when it wouldn't fire those weird shots. He got to him. The man with the blue eyes and ripped up clothing tackled his father. Noel looked at Sau one last time. White-Cell looked far out as he saw the young boy watching. Laughing, he sliced Noel up and down. Raymundo kept pulling his teary eyed brother to keep running.

I haven't felt this alive in ages. Now it's onto the kid.

"Wait, White-Cell. Don't leave us wounded like this." He looked over. Wishing he didn't bring his weak counterparts. He knew he had to help them because his army isn't so big anymore.

"I'll get you for this!" He yelled, lifting both hands into the sky. "You will join me Sau Titan!!!"

Hard lifestyle

Ray sat on the bench stump with his sobbing brother in his arms. The ship gently rocking in the night, the soft slashing of water seemed to haunt the mind of Raymundo. He was there to lose his mother, and he saw his father ripped to shreds. No more parents in this cold world, just him and Sau.

"Ray, why did those men kill dad?" Sau asked as he began to sob again.

"I don't know Sau. I wish I did but I don't."

"Where are we going to live?" Sau now looked up as Ray looked down. From this angle he looked just like his mother, which hurt him even more.

"Don't worry about that, leave it to me. Get some rest Sau, we have some long days ahead of us."

Raymundo woke up to his foot being kicked. The bright sun blinded him before he saw the driver of the fish boat.

"Alright kids, we're on Kaimana beach and I have to drop you off. Have to grab the fish bright and early." Ray woke up Sau as they headed off the boat and walked the beach.

"Ray, I'm hungry." Sau said as his stomach rumbled. They didn't have any money, didn't have a plan. Raymundo knew that if he didn't think quick, they'd be sleeping outside during the night.

"Once we get off this beach I'll get us something to eat." They walked up the dock from the sand to the concrete. Both knowing their bodies reeked of fish as people who walked past them scrunched up their noses.

"What's that big building, with the red and white paint?" Sau pointed at the building across the street from them.

"That's a church, meaning they are Christian of some sort." Ray took note of the people coming out, it must be sunday service.

"Do you think they have food? Maybe they can help us with some place to sleep." Ray nodded to appease his little brother. He knew even at that young age, the world doesn't work like that. Even if people claim to be Christian, most of them were Haole. Their father always told them to be weary of the Haole's on the island.

"Yeah, come with me." The brothers crossed the street towards the church. Heading inside, only people that were left were the elderly who wanted to talk with the choir and pastor. Within a couple of seconds, the few people that were in the church started to notice the boys.

"May I help you?" A man who didn't look like a pastor came up with a woman Raymundo figured to be his wife.

"Our father was," Ray abruptly put his hand in Sau's chest to hush him.

"We're homeless. We're just looking for a place to sleep and food." The couple looked at each other like they'd hit the jackpot.

"Honey, if we take in these two boys the state would give us double the money." The woman whispered to the man. He smiled then squatted down to shake both the boys hands.

"What are your names?"

"I'm Raymundo, and this is my little brother Sau."

"You can call us Mr. and Mrs. Aweo. You can stay with us for the night, get you boys some food. Maybe talk about things long term. Help you kids out, as devout Christians that is our job." Ray accepted as did Sau. However, Sau looked into the eyes of the couple. He didn't like the feeling they gave off, but thoughts of his dad filled his mind. The brothers followed the couple to their car, almost as if this was the start of their new life.

Within a year of staying with the Roman Catholic older Hawaiian couple, the brothers were enrolled at a new school and had to adjust from being country boys, to urban lifestyle.

"Sau, you okay?" Raymundo asked as they were on the school bus.

"I guess." Sau stared outside. Big tall buildings, going to an inner city school. Ray kept a slight gaze on his little brother.

"I'm still hurting too Sau, but don't worry, we'll be alright" They pulled up to their K-12 school, and looked at all the kids piling to the front door. "Once we get inside, I have to head to the middle school wing. You should know where your classes are though. I won't be home from school right away, tryouts for the cross country team are always on the first day I guess."

Everything was new. The marble walls. He was used to seeing brown kids in overalls and boots. At least half the people he saw were Haole. Their milky skin and tight jean pants seemed odd to him. Or seeing the black boys with bulky shoes with three white lines going down the side of them. He looked but couldn't make sense of so many A's and D's in the word. Once he entered the elementary wing, a thought had hit him like it hadn't in a while. *My dad still isn't here.*

Sau got off of the cheese yellow bus and walked home to his two story house. The car in the driveway indicated that *they* were home. Sau walked in and knew what to expect by now.

"Sau! Didn't I tell you to mop the floor?" His host mother yelled coming into the living room as he walked in the house. Sau stared at her blankly. "Answer me!" Still no words. "Are you feeling proud today?" "I have nothing but pride in me." He answered.

"Lord Jesus. Boy that's a deadly sin. Don't worry, if it's in you, I'll beat it out of you." She pulled out her oiled leather belt. With fear, he ran upstairs and she followed. He tried to close the door but she overpowered him. Slash after slash she whipped him. He tried to run but she grabbed his long medium length hair. His breathing got heavier before he reached for the door handle. Another slash, his fingers made contact with an electrical outlet. Suddenly he was pulled to the ground, waiting for another slash that wouldn't come. He looked up and saw his host mother spazzing out of control while still holding his wrist.

"Mrs. Aweo, are you alright?" He asked. Slowly, he loosened her grip and let her hand fall to the ground. Still slightly shaking. "I'm calling for help." Sau ran downstairs to the kitchen to dial 9-1-1.

"What happened to Mrs. Aweo?" Raymundo rushed into the hospital with Mr. Aweo. Sau stood up with the detective.

"She got electrocuted." The detective said.

"Well why are you here?" Raymundo scanned the area. Never liking hospitals since the day his mother had passed away.

"Just to see if there was any foul play. Sau and your father here,"

"Host parent." Raymundo corrected.

"Right, now that he's here we can talk with him because your brother here isn't saying much." The doctor came out of the operating room. As Mr. Aweo went in to check on his wife.

"Well okay it seems like your host mother is fine. She just needs some recovery time because of the shock, but all in all, she's okay."

"Thank goodness." Ray sighed. "Detective, thanks for showing up but I don't think any foul play was involved." The detective nodded and walked towards the coffee machine.

"Young man I don't know the circumstances." Multiple wrinkles forming on the doctor's bald head. "Her body doesn't show any marks from electrical cords. It's quite a scenario." Ray looked down at his brother then back up.

"Quite a mystery huh? Excuse us." Ray moved his brother away awkwardly. "Alright Sau, time to speak up." Sau looked down and hesitated.

"I touched an outlet, like where we plug in our MP3 chargers. And then suddenly she was on the ground." Sau said, not really having an idea how it happened.

"I guess you're too young for magic tricks. This is something real." Raymundo got to thinking. Then he remembered what had caught his eye the day his mom died. He thought it was the sweat getting in his eyes from working out but he had to be sure. "I remember the day that had happened to dad. You were doing something that I saw with my own eyes, but thought it was just the sweat in my eyes. Can you snap your fingers for me?" Raymundo asked. Sau made sure no one was looking. He snapped his fingers while small sparks were flying out.

"It started happening the day dad died." Ray looked into his brother's fearful eyes.

"Don't be scared. I need you to do me a big favor. Keep this between us. I can't prove it, but I bet it has something to do with that stuff they put into you as a baby." He couldn't find the word for it.

"I'll keep it a secret Ray. I just didn't mean to hurt her." The doctor abruptly came out.

"Raymundo, she requested to see you and only you. Sau, Mr. Aweo will come out."

'I'll go." Raymundo said. As he left Mr. Aweo came out.

"You okay Sau?"

"I don't know."

"What did you tell your brother."

"Just how she fell out of nowhere."

"Good. Last thing we need is you running your mouth."

"Mrs. Aweo hit me. With a belt."

"I know, one thing we don't have in my house is children with sinful pride. If we tell you to do something then do it. You were nothing but homeless children when we found you. You belong to us."

"I am Sau Titan. My father told me I am my own man."

"Your father can't even help you with your multiplication. Don't play with me."

"When someone walks in, I'm telling them what she did to me."

"Oh yeah, well you try that. I'll split you and your brother up." Sau thought and cried. Mr. Aweo smiled knowing he got himself his own little prize. "You have the devil inside of you. I don't believe you're innocent. But you don't have to tell me. I'll always find out. I'm watching you, you little bastard. Something isn't right."

"Fine. I won't tell."

"Good boy." He got up and walked to the door. "And Sau, Raymundo better not find out."

Sorrow With Friendly Faces

Sau stood in the front of the classroom of tenth grade history honors. With one more paragraph to read from his paper, he took a deep breath and continued speaking.

"Malcolm X changed his views of the white man when he made his pilgrimage to Mecca, Saudi Arabia. The Islamic capital of the world. Sitting next to Blacks, whites, Asians, and Indians. He realized every man, white, black, yellow, and red. They were his Muslim brothers." Sau put his paper down to signal that he was done with his "How Knowledge Changes People essay."

"Absolutely great Sau." Mr. Howard emerged from his chair. "Hand in your paper and please take your seat." Sau put it in the basket and went to sit while the other student began to talk.

"Yo Sau, you trying out for the football team today?" He turned to see a freckled face haole boy staring him down.

"Yes I am."

"Cool. We have this thing called freshman friday. All of us upperclassmen just break down the freshman as we build them up for the season. Starts at three."

"I'll pass on that." Sau turned around and shook his head. Beating on the weak was never something that sat right with him. The loud thunder from outside put a nervous feeling in his stomach. But as the day went on it slowly went away.

Throughout the school days he would just stay to himself. A few conversations here and there. But nothing that was too important. He was a lonely kid. Often spending all of his time with Raymundo when he wasn't working. And when work did take Ray away, Sau was just left at home with homework and thoughts. And experimenting here and there with snapping electricity out of his fingers. He never really cared that he could do it, thinking of it as a redundant magic trick. Not caring to know why he could make such a thing happen.

As the bell rang for dismissal, Sau made his way to the locker room to get ready for practice. His sophomore year. This would be the time colleges would start looking at high school players. His dream was to stay on the island and play for the Hawaii Warriors. However, this being his first year, he had a long way to go.

"We have a new islander to help beat down the freshman." Sau didn't turn but knew the haole was talking to him. "Say boy, as soon as they walk in, you and the other islanders go first."

"I'm not a boy. And you don't tell me what to do. You're taking a small tradition and turning it purely violent. Seems lame to me haole."

"You know what's lame. A no named islander who thinks he's different from the rest. Know your place boy." Sau's anger was being tested by the minute. He wanted to lash out but knew to never throw the first punch on school grounds. So he just slowly took off his school clothes to get changed for practice.

"Geez Sau. You are cut up with muscles, not a piece of fat anywhere on you. Why haven't you been playing sports?" Another haole asked.

"I know why." The trouble maker started. "Because he's probably too busy helping his father farm for us *haoles* on the island, isn't that right Sau?" Sau threw the bench he was sitting on with tremendous force. All the boys backed up. His rage fuming out as he focused on the trouble maker.

"Say it again." He whispered to himself. "Say it again!" This time he screamed.

"Maybe you are different islander, you're a freak." Sau's eyes began to glow yellow. Sparks began to fly off his body as the lights in the locker room exploded as the boys went into a frenzy. Realizing he was in too deep, he panicked and slowly walked out of the darkness. Leaving the locker room he ran out behind the school to calm down. The heavy rain and wind didn't help him but he felt as if he couldn't show his face back in the school.

"Why did I get out of control?" He muttered to himself. He knew when to control his temper. Why couldn't he today? The loud thunder and the lightning didn't help either. The rain made it hard to see anywhere. Getting out his track phone, he had to call Ray.

"What's up brother? Wait, aren't you trying out for the team today?"

"No. Ray. I'm scared. You have to come pick me up from school."

"Sau it's hard for me to leave the office. And plus it's storming outside like crazy."

"Please Ray. You know that electrical stuff from my fingertips you told me to keep a secret? Well I got angry and some people saw it. But it was coming off of my body instead of my fingertips. That's never happened before, Ray please pick me up."

"Damn, alright. Just stay right there. Here I come."

Unexpecting Situation

The storm hadn't let up. Sau wondered if there was a hurricane warning. He even noticed the football team went back into the school when the rain got too hectic.

"Come on Ray where are you?" The temperature began to drop significantly. Through the fog, he saw headlights and the familiar red Nissan. "Thank God." As Sau ran towards his brother's car, the loud thunder seemed to be at a constant rumble. Sau had stopped a few feet before the car. Looking up at the sky, the lightning seemed to be moving in slow motion. A mesmerized Sau awed at the scene as it seemed to pull him in. He couldn't hear the rumbling thunder anymore. Or the honking of the horn from his brother's direction.

"Sau, what the hell are you doing?" Raymundo noticed the more frequent lightning strikes. Sau, still dazed, felt like he was in euphoria. Without thought he automatically snapped his fingers, as the energy of the lightning strikes around him exploded leaving a yellow haze. "Sau, get in the damn car!"

"Why does this feel so good?" Sau said to himself. Still in that euphoric daze from the explosion. Feeling as if he controlled the lightning.

"Sau, I'm getting out. What is happening to you?" Ray unbuckled his seatbelt ready to advance until he saw electricity spewing out of Sau's body. Sau looked in Ray's direction as it had taken him aback. Ray wasn't looking into his little brothers' brown pupils. His irises were filled with yellow streaks. A smile on his face. Suddenly the feeling faded and Sau regained his normal self.

"What the," Before Sau could finish, he stretched out his arms as a flash of yellow light shot from his body. A strong sound of thunder following. As Ray uncovered his eyes, he felt sheer horror looking at his brother's lifeless body.

"No!" Ray ran out and carried him to the car. He laid his wet body across the backseat and immediately drove in the direction of the hospital. "Stay with me Sau." Ray kept looking back and forth, focusing on the road while shaking Sau here and there to make sure he was still alive. "Come on, get out of the way." Even though he was an experienced driver, Ray had a difficult time avoiding cars and red lights while going so far above the speed limit.

"Ah." Sau slowly regained consciousness. Raymundo turned and saw his brother rubbing his eyes. Not focusing on the road, he was blinded by the semi truck coming head on. Sau perked his head up, as if time moved slow for him, he jumped through the windshield and ran head on towards the truck.

"Sau!" Ray screamed before Sau made contact with the truck. He sat at the wheel with his mouth wide open. Not believing what he just saw. Sau loosened his grip on the front rungs and realized what he had done. He had stopped a semi truck by ramming himself into the front bumper. Looking back at Ray, he didn't know how he just did that. All he saw was the truck, then doing what he had to do to stop the crash.

"Jesus Sau!" As the oncoming traffic came to a halt, people started to get out of their cars in dismay of what they just saw.

"Did that boy just stop the truck?"

"He would be dead if that truck had hit him."

"Look at what he did to the truck." Sau had heard all of the people's remarks. Panicking, he ignored his brother's car and ran in the direction of his house.

"What. The. Hell." Raymundo said before he saw Sau zoom down the street at lightning fast speed. Sau wasn't even aware of how fast he was going until he was passing cars with ease speeding past the speed limit. That scared him more as he began running faster.

"Jesus Christ." Sau reached his house in no time as he went straight to his room. Not noticing his clothes were drenched with a mixture of rain and sweat.

"Sau!" Raymundo barged through the front door a few minutes later.

"No Ray. Not right now." He locked the door.

"Come on man, it's me. You don't have to fear me."

"I don't fear you Ray. I fear myself. I always could spark electricity, but what the hell? Look at me. Look at what I just did."

"Listen dude, what I saw was something out of a sci-fi movie. My best guess is that it has something to do with what they put in you as a baby."

"What? What did they put in me as a baby?" Sau opened up the door and was face to face with him.

"I forget the name, but it resembles plutonium. And plutonium only gets stronger as it ages, as with you. Like when you were young you could only snap electric. That was when you were younger. Now, sparks are flying off of you, plus I saw electricity in your eyes."

"The lightning strikes were hitting the ground near me. Being engulfed in that haze, it was just too surreal."

"You passed out from it."

"Yeah, but I was conscious. Restoring energy I feel. Come on Ray, you have to have some memory of the name of that supplement. I need to know what is happening with my own body." Raymundo ran to the computer and quickly typed. Typing for anything that'll jog his memory.

"Uh? Oh, Dad said it to me one time. Electorpais!" Ray typed the name into the browser. "Nothing on that word, but here is something about just *Pais*. Banned in 1913, the supplement Pais is a sparked stimulant. Physical Characteristics says it looks like a metallic rock. But not rare to be used with a needle. The compound resembles Plutonium, a lasting energy that gets stronger over time."

"That makes sense." Sau started. "Sparked stimulant, read more."

"It says the last man was injected with it in his arm in December of 1912 in Pasadena California. He showed great strength, lifting up cars in a police standoff before he was shot in the head. Since June of the following year, the supplement was declared illegal in the contiguous United States."

"So not Alaska and Hawaii. They weren't states yet." Sau turned whispering. "He was injected in his arm, so he had great strength. I was injected in my foot, so I run fast. Maybe strength comes along with it.

When I was seven, I started to spark. I always could do that but the distance got farther by every year.

Until I could zap it when I was eleven. Now I'm sixteen, and it went to sparks flying off of my whole body.

Before the haze."

"Yeah, from what I saw. Your reaction time, speed and strength changed since the haze. It makes you get stronger over time. Right there it says it's a spark stimulant. So maybe that's where the electricity comes in. But why did dad always tell me about Electorpais instead of just Pais."

"Damn ray. So that means I'm stronger than him. It's been built in me for sixteen years. My instincts must also be above average thar

"'Wait, here's something." Raymundo clicked on another link. "The government tested the Electorpais again in 1958. In Hawaii. It was still legal because the following year Hawaii became the fiftieth state."
"Who'd they test it on?"

"Apes. Since humans share the closest DNA with them on this earth. It says here that in the following years, they experienced cat-like reactions. Genetic mutations to their physical appearance. Increased speed and strength. And," Ray paused as his eyes went big. "Extreme aggression. And Violent rage. They tested it on three Apes. The most violent one ended up killing the other two. And that Ape was put down shortly after the procedure was compromised." Sau remembered his flash of anger with Mrs. Aweo from his childhood. Then to when he threw the bench in the locker room.

"We've seen all of those in me, but rage? Violence. Ray, I'm not that type of guy. I'm not an animal. Apes are animals, some things don't always transfer over, right?" Ray sat in silence avoiding Sau's nervous stare.

"Just keep staying on the right path bro. It'll be alright. We will be alright."

White-Cell stood while he talked to the unidentified man on the screen. A black and red hood covering the top half of his face. The rest of the Seekers surrounded White-Cell.

"White-Cell." The man spoke in a slow and mischievous voice. "As you know, the business I got into last week has scorched my face. Once the healing process is over, I'll be making my way back off the mainland. You know how I am with making an entrance. Give it about a week or so."

"Yes I do. Now what happens to be the purpose of this call?" White-Cell asked.

"This is about the decision you made about sixteen years ago. Using our precious resources we stole from the government to use for your own selfish good." White-Cell gulped. "I'm not mad at you. You made a decision, so you have to stick with it. Have you found the boy since you lost track of him?"

"No, I haven't. We're still on the big island looking for him."

"The seekers are an organization of strong beings who represent the powers of Pais. The small supplement you put in the boy is needed. Are you sure you can continue leading this expedition? It's been years upon years since you lost contact."

"Don't you worry. I will track him down sooner rather than later."

"Damn right you will, because if you don't, that throws two decades worth of work in the trash."

"Like I said. Don't you worry. He is still in Hawaii. I feel it."

Chump Change

"So this is what you really want?" Raymundo asked.

"Yes, school ain't for me. It never was. Especially since what happened with those jocks, rumors about me will spread."

"I don't like this Sau. You need a high school education in this world. That diploma gets you the most simplest jobs."

"I can find a way to make money if need be, trust me. I can spend the first couple of weeks just chilling before I truly have to. Or maybe," Sau paused at his thoughts.

"Maybe what?"

"Maybe I can use my abilities for good." Sau smiled as he looked down. "To help people."

"I hope you're not talking about being some sort of hero."

"No, not a hero. A superhero." They now both looked at each other with opposite facial expressions to the idea.

"No. Get that stupid little thought out of your head. This is real life Sau, not some action movie. This is real life with real criminals who have guns. There are also ones who are not afraid to gundown some teenager in some flappy costume."

"See, you're making it sound like this is some superhero story. Think about it, since Honolulu blue PD ceased, the police department here is complete shit. What was the percent? Over sixty percent of petty criminals get away with their crimes. That's more than half. And who's not to say that a petty crime can end up with a kid dying. Or someone having their life altered in the most negative way. Or a father dying in front of his kids." Raymundo picked up what Sau's last sentence was truly about.

"You're thinking emotionally. This all has to do with dad. You want to be a hero so no one has to go through with what we both went through. Your heart's in the right place. But you have to understand, bad things happen to everyone. Whether you're a good or bad person."

"Ray." Sau shook his head. "Yes, that has something to do with it. But it's my choice."

"You're also looking for ones responsible for killing our dad. You won't run into them Sau. They're gone."

"But they're still out there." He now walked over to the window. "Who's to say they haven't done that to so many other families? Sometimes, I sit up at night. And think about what would happen if I ever saw them." Sparks started sparking off of Sau.

"Um, brother."

"I don't know what I'll do when I see them. But I do know how it's gonna end."

"Sau!" Raymundo caught his attention. "You were sparking everywhere."

"Guess my powers are mixed in with my emotions."

"Alright brother, here is the deal. I don't like it, but if you're a man like you say, you have to live with the consequences. You don't wanna go to school? Fine. But you won't sit on your ass all day. Living with some fantasy of being a help to the people. You're a man of your word right? Alright, so be out there where the help is needed. In downtown Honolulu. That's where the crime rate is booming. Don't get it twisted, what you see on Tv isn't what's going to happen out there. It'll be boring and slow paced. Now think about it before you choose." Sau sat back in deep thought

"I need a mask. Something to cover my face. Can you get me something from your fabric company that I can see out of?" Ray nodded and took in a couple breaths. "Also, I don't know how to truly work my powers. Can you help me?"

"Dude, I'm regular. How am I supposed to help you with something I don't know about? I don't want to teach you something wrong and it ends up being your downfall.

"Alright, I'll figure it out on my own. But I tell you this, our lives are gonna change forever."

"Last time our lives changed was when our dad died."

Sau wasn't used to the fast pace of Downtown Honolulu. He'd never seen so many stores aligned on just one block. Being there on "patrol" for the past few days didn't do him any good in adjusting to the new environment.

"What am I doing?" He asked himself. Raymundo was right. It wasn't like the movies where you would instantly find crime. Defeated, Sau decided he would live a normal life. He'd only missed a couple days of school, no big deal. Before running home, he stepped into the corner store to find something quick to eat.

"I want the money. Now!" Sau looked at the man in a leather jacket holding a gun to the cashier. He stood still at the door. The woman stood frightened shaking uncontrollably. "Do you hear me! Give me the money!" He yelled. The girl handed him a glass jar of coins.

"This is all I have sir. We didn't m-make a lot of donations today." She stuttered holding the jar.

"Coins? You think I want coins?" He cocked his gun. With a fraction of a second, Sau ran and had the man up in the air, right before slamming him down. The gun went off and shot the light in the ceiling. The sparks flew down and triggered something in Sau.

"You coward!" He pulled the robber up with one hand. All juiced. "You were going to shoot this woman over chump change!" He shocked the man for two seconds. The blonde in his long hair standing up from the electricity.

"The police are on their way." The girl said. Sau looked at her as she trembled with the phone in her hand.

"Damn." She saw his face. Raymundo still hadn't found Sau a mask yet. "He won't be going anywhere any time soon." He then looked at the robber still having short spasms.

"Sir, how did you get here so quick and, oh my god." She rested her hands on the glass counter. "Who are you?" She looked up. Sau stared back into her brown eyes and saw something. Trust. And an idea, like he'd never thought of pop into his head.

"Lightning Striker."

The Unofficial Declared Secret

"Ray!" Sau yelled coming into the house.

"What?" He answered from the kitchen.

"I stopped a robber today. Man it was crazy. Then guess what. When a light shattered, sparks came out and I got stronger. I can use electricity as a power man. Isn't that great?" Ray came from the back and looked at Sau. "What?"

"Check this." Ray opened up a duffle bag and tossed items of clothing to him. "One of my high school buddies owed me a favor. He works at Uniform Express. Told him to make a free order for me." Sau studied the clothes. The mask. The tight compression bodysuit. The light blue, black, and yellow lightning stripes appealed to him in an awe moment way.

"Ray, what does this mean?"

"It means you're a hero. A superhero officially."

"Unofficial. You know cause no one knows who I am yet." They both laughed. "Lightning Striker." Sau whispered.

"You say something?"

"That's who I am. Lightning Striker. King of Hawaii." Ray chuckled again.

"Slow your roll. You still don't know how to fully use your powers. I'll say it again. Be careful Sau. Just like heroes there are villains."

It Happens

"Any findings on the boy?" White-cell asked one of his seekers.

"No sir. But we have to think logically. We've scanned this whole Island for some years now. We have to relocate. Or just find a few more people for the army. Any more of that electrical component based electorpais you've put in the boy?"

"I can't! I can't think logically. That boy has a power in him that belongs to me. All of the electrical supplements I had is in the boy now. And there is no more electorpais left. Only way to get the power now is a blood transfusion." White-Cell got off his chair and paced his underground lair. "So let's say I go along with this plan. Where would he be? Hypothetically?"

"Well, seeing as he went off as a boy, I highly doubt he left the islands. Maybe, just maybe he's on Oahu." White-Cell looked astonished at his seeker.

"Szcar. You're Brilliant. The highest population in Hawaii. Easy to blend in. Tell the others to have my things ready tomorrow morning. We're gonna capture him." He started to leave.

"Sir, what if he doesn't want to join us?" White-Cell looked back with malicious intent.

"Trust me, he will. For if he doesn't, I'll kill his brother too."

"Just be calm. You'll be alright." Raymundo said through the phone.

"It's my first night watch. And there are a lot of sketchy people in the city." Sau whispered back. He looked out onto the dark street with some people on it. The ominous yellow streetlights made their shadows grow. So far, he'd missed a couple weeks of school, figuring it would be too late to go back.

"If you're lucky you'll have a boring night. And if you don't, no one in this world has the powers you have.

You just have to know what you're doing with them."

"Yeah I guess." Sau rubbed his face through his mask. The trench coat he wore covered up the rest of his suit.

"Oh crap, I let the fire for the Tilapia get too high."

"Try not to burn the house down Mr.Chef." Sau looked out across the street as the store owner for a jewelry shop was locking up his shop. He was about to look away before two tall figures approached the man in a threatening manner. "Got to go Ray, looks like my night isn't gonna be boring."

"Wait, Sau, what's going on-" Sau hung up and watched what was going on. The figures had baggy clothes on and kept pointing their fingers at the old man.

"Help! These robbers are-" The old man tried to yell but was pistol whipped onto the ground. Taking his keys, they opened up the store.

"Show time." Sau took off his coat and zoomed into the store.

"Man we hit the motherload. If I wasn't gonna be rich, I would've felt bad for laying that old hag out."

"You never lie, Taylor. Aye, look for the diamond ear-" the one guy turned and saw Sau. "Whoa Taylor look!" The both stared in amusement.

"You cowards beat up an old defenseless man. For some jewelry you were too broke to pay for?" Sau began walking closer.

"Man let's waste this dick!" Taylor who seemed to be in charge yelled. He pulled his gun out but was pushed into the glass case with the necklaces. The other guy tried to wrap Sau up, but Sau ran backwards into the ring display case.

"It could've been easier for you two." He picked up the guy and tied his belt to the fire extinguisher plug.

"Shut up, you fake wannabe hero." Taylor walked and stood toe to toe with him. Gun cocked in his hand.

"You're strong, but nothing compared to a hot bullet. It'll be a shame to have your loved ones bury you.

Faking to be something you never were." In an instant, Sau threw Taylor through the glass shop window. The alarms sounded as Sau stood over him.

"Never talk about a man's family." Grabbing him by the jacket sleeve, Sau tied it with the other sleeve between his legs. "Are you ok?" He said helping the old man up.

"It's quite alright young ma-" he paused and looked at the guy who was helping him. "I take it you're someone who likes his privacy."

"Yeah, I am."

"Well, you're in the direct line of the camera." He pointed to the corner of the store and Sau stared frightened as the red light was on. "Even if they robbed me, they wouldn't have got away. But thanks young man." Sau nodded and sped off as he heard sirens in the distance.

"That's the problem with Honolulu now. So many people are trying to live this so-called thug life." Raymundo complained.

"But still, I was in perfect view of the camera. And plus the police came. Oh man Ray, what're we gonna do?"

"Was your face out in the open?"

"No, I had everything on."

"Then it's alright. It'll be on YouTube or something. Hit some views and then die out within three months."

"Are you sure?"

"Nothing is ever certain Sau, but I'm almost positive." Sau looked desperate.

"How positive is that almost?"

"Sau! You're overreacting, it's fine. Get some sleep." Sau nodded as Raymundo called it a night and went to his room. Thinking about what just transpired, he realized he could react under pressure. A gun didn't scare him in the heat of the moment.

"I can't believe how fast I'm changing." Sau took a couple deep breaths before finally relaxing. This was his life now. Around a month ago was his last day attending school. Now, as he laid down on his couch, he smiled as he could truthfully say, "I am a hero."

Blown Party Events

"I'm not staying another night in this hotel, I want my lair." White-Cell complained.

"Sir. We did what you've asked. It's only been a couple weeks. Watch something to preoccupy your mind." Szcar turned on the TV and flipped through the channels.

"Wait, go back." White-Cell saw something that intrigued his mind as Szcar turned back to the news.

"Now in breaking news, there was an attempted armed robbery at the jewelry store in downtown Honolulu. The teenagers in fact are high school standouts in their respective sports. The news today isn't about the robbers, however. It's actually about what the camera caught during the save. As you're looking now it shows a person in a mask stopping the criminals, and helping up the old man. The hero showed great speed and agility in tying up the robbers. To the unidentifiable character, the city of Honolulu owes you a thank you."

"It's him. It's the boy. It has to be." White-Cell smiled.

"How can you be so sure?"

"Think about it, great speed and agility. And not to mention, he's in Hawaii, what are the chances of that? The boy and his brother must've moved to the big city. I gotta think. If he stops crimes at alerts, we have to alert him. Do a big crime."

"What do you have in mind?" White-Cell looked at Szcar and gave him a devious smile.

"Gather our things, long time no see for our boy turned hero."

"So explain to me again why I have to go to this party that you're invited to."

"First off Sau, it's not a party. It's a get together in the Warrior square."

"Warrior Square? I've been wanting to go there since we got here."

"Changed your mind now huh? Listen, there's gonna be a couple hundred people there. You may lose me in the mix, but I have to talk to some colleagues. So just enjoy yourself, and comb your hair." Ray messed his little brother's hair up again. Both smiling while getting ready.

"Why did you wear such a baggy polo?" Raymundo asked.

"I have my suit on under. I just had a feeling to bring it. Hey, why do they call it a Warrior square if it's not shaped like a square?"

"Beats me. I'm just trying to push through this crown before I knock these rude assholes out." Ray pushed through grinding his teeth.

"I'm gonna hang back, enjoy the view." Ray kept going forward as Sau looked all around him. The scenery was something spectacular to his eyes. Big tall buildings for government uses. People of the rich going around like they belong here, mostly haole people. A few Hawaiians mingled around, but most are servers. Talk about equality.

"Boy, another cocktail?" Sau turned around to a middle aged woman with her hair looking like that tall ancient building that tilts. "Oh for god sakes I'm sorry, this boy doesn't speak English." She whispered too loudly to what seemed like her fat spouse. She motioned like pouring something into her empty class then stared me down.

"Oh I know what this means." Sau smiled. He held out his knuckle and slowly raised his middle finger to them. "There's a cocktail for you." He went along about his business, giving up on finding his brother any time soon. An eerie feeling came up his neck as his senses started going off the fritz.

"Oh my god what is that!" Someone screamed. Everyone turned their attention to the balcony of the government office. There stood a man with long white hair, white and black armor. Sau felt as if he saw the man somewhere previously, but where? People screamed again as he grabbed the police commissioner and dangled him over the edge.

"First big one." Sau said to himself as he sped off to change. A quick Change of outfit, he put on his mask and started to run alongside the surface of other buildings to get to the villain. His attention was diverted

when he dropped the commissioner. "Crap." Sau jumped and wrapped his arms around the commissioner to protect him. Hitting the ground in a thud, and leaving a path of broken concrete in the way. Sau looked up and saw the man smiling at him.

It was him. The boy. White-Cell remembered his eyes just like those of a kid. He jumped off the building and landed feet first. Slowly walking towards Sau.

"So we finally meet. You have any idea who I am?" White-Cell mocked.

"Some lunatic who thinks he's gonna take over Hawaii." White-Cell laughed.

"I'm not gonna take over Hawaii, not yet at least. Baby Steps!!" He jumped and kicked Sau in the chest.

Sending him back a few feet. "I'm white-Cell by the way."

"Police! Stop!" A couple police officers held the two at gunpoint. "You're under arrest! Both of you. You have the right to-" White-Cell sounded his beam at the officers causing them to drop. He looked and fell back at Sau's punch.

"I'm Lightning Striker. Hero of Hawaii."

Sau wished he didn't tell him his hero name, but the arrogance took over him. White-cell stood up and braced for a fight.

"Let's see what you got." They ran at each other and jumped. Sau tackling White-Cell causing them to wrestle. Throwing body blows, Sau started getting the upper hand.

"Looks like it's an easy win." Sau boasted. He jumped and threw his leg at him. White-Cell caught it, causing Sau to drop.

"Enjoy the ride." He ignited the boosts in his boots and took off. Sau's upper body flying all over the place, crashing into the rock parts of buildings. Hitting flag poles and arches before he flung Sau through the glass of the court house. Trying to stand, Sau briefly looked up before White-Cell kicked him to the judges stand. "Please don't tell me the fights over." Sau wiped blood from his mouth.

"Oh my friend White-Cell, it has only begun."

Sau dazed White-Cell with a punch again. So fast that White-Cell couldn't see until he was hit with a table, then punched through the other glass to the balcony.

"We'd make a great team Lightning Striker."

"You're crazy if you think I would join you." Sau tried to grab him but White-Cell elbowed him in the groin.

"We will definitely have this conversation again, but I have to go. I hope I didn't do too much damage, you'll probably be able to reproduce." He stuck a knife in the stone, jumped then blasted away. In a matter of seconds, the knife exploded.

Sau's vision was hazy but he began to snap out of it. He heard a blast and soon was free falling. Seeing clearly now, he saw two children right under him where he was falling.

"Watch out!" It was no use, he was still too high up for them to hear his voice. He kept snapping his fingers but nothing came out. Taking off a glove, he quickly saw it was hard rubber. Coming closer to the ground, he shot electricity out from his palms at the children. Shielding them in an energy force field as he landed next to them breaking in the concrete.

"Wow, a superhero. Who are you?" The little boy with the dirty blonde hair asked. Sau gazed out in the crowd that gathered. Everyone in amazement at what they've just seen.

"Name is Lightning Striker buddy." Sau turned to see police men on his right.

"Thanks for saving the children." The commissioner accommodated. Sau nodded and saw Raymundo smiling from behind them. Quickly, he sped out of there almost like a blur. Inside him was a feeling he hasn't felt since being a kid, happiness.

Midnight Star

Sau had been sitting on the couch for a couple hours, waiting for Raymundo to come home. He kept replaying the images in his head. The words, the little boys congratulating him. He finally felt important, like he really mattered. To save someone's life. Not just the kids, but the whole family.

"Hey bro." Ray came stumbling in. His dress shirt unbuttoned and the tie loose.

"I didn't even hear you come in." Sau chuckled and stared down his brother. "Looks like you had a lot to drink. Wish you didn't drive home like that."

"You're right, I am sorry. It's just a celebration. After you left, everyone kept going on about how you're the new hero. My baby brother, seems like that black heart you've always had is fading away." Ray plopped himself on the couch.

"Black heart? What does that mean?"

"Oh Sau please. Man you've been depressed and sad ever since dad died. You've been so angry. Now you have nothing to worry about. As have I but we channel our emotions differently. Aye, flick on the news." Sau chuckled again at Ray's slurred words.

"Sure thing. But before I do, you gave me rubber gloves. Rubber and electricity doesn't make a spark."

"My bad, can we talk about this later? My head is spinning."He turned onto the news, and immediately saw what the topic was going to be.

"In most recent news, just a few hours ago we had a little brawl between good and evil. The same hero who we now know as Lightning Striker, from the jewelry store video came out again to save the police commissioner and children in Warrior Square today. What is most shocking is the one man behind this. White-Cell as he calls himself. As you see here he is dangling the commissioner over the edge. Police have a warrant for his arrest and a reward for whoever turns him in. I'm Alberta Chaney, and this is channel eight news." Sau sat back and gathered up his thoughts.

"Damn Ray. They know me, they love me. They just-." Sau turned and saw Raymundo passed out on the couch. "Goodnight brother."

"I guess he saved the children, lucky little man."

"Sir, why didn't you just capture him and make him work with us?"

"I have to see his face, then I make my move. He won't have a front to put on while he is out of character." White-Cell took off his mask. *"He's stronger than I thought, but he doesn't know himself. He could have easily killed me and not break a sweat. This is good. Now we have the upper hand."*

"How so?"

"We can beat him in his weak spots. And Trust me, there is an evil in every person. We make him see the way, the true way of us people in our darkest form. The right way. That type of power on the seekers? With his power, we can have world domination."

"Your Cleverness is inspirational sir."

"This city is only so big. I will see him soon. Soon enough."

A Run-In

Sau needed gloves that could conduct electricity. Rubber ones stopped his electrical flow through his fingertips.

"Think Sau think, what is a conductor of electricity?" He said to himself. Trying to remember what school had taught him. Walking downtown, he looked at a billboard and saw two athletes on it. Advertising copper fit arm bands. Copper, that is a conductor of electricity. He went to the sporting gloves store to get copper gloves.

"Can I help you sir?" A lady in a ponytail asked. Sau briefly hesitated before answering.

"Um yes, the copper fit section?"

"We had a new shipment this morning, aisle nine on the left." She pointed as he went in the direction.

"Yes." He spoke to himself. He found the perfect blue glove with the black copper lining on the side. He went to cash out and accidentally bumped into someone. "My bad dude."

"It's quite alright." A chill went up Sau's spine. He looked up to see those piercing blue eyes. And with that voice, he recognized it from yesterday. Somewhere else he can't put his finger on. He soon realized that the guy didn't know what he looked like under the mask. Sau paid for his stuff and went to the back of the store to change. Slightly keeping his eyes on White-Cell making sure he didn't lose him. Once in appropriate gear, he walked up behind him as everyone in the store gasped noticing the hero.

"What are you doing here?" Sau braced for a fight. White-Cell turned around and smiled.

"Wow, not even two minutes later and you blow your cover. I was expecting you to wait until I got outside. But changing in the back of the store? Come on Lightning Striker, please tell me you're smarter than that." Sau felt like a fool. The mask only mattered to the crowd, White-Cell knew what he looked like. He must've followed him.

"I might've blown my cover, but I can whip your ass like I did yesterday." White-Cell chuckled at Sau's insult. The two are oblivious to the entire store watching the confrontation.

"How're we going to do this? Have a nice talk? Or end up with me wiping the floor with you, and have you miss out on what I planned." Sau contemplated with himself. Knowing that even if he was being led into a trap, he'd have to take the risk to see if White-Cell reveals any key information.

"What do you wanna talk about?"

"Do you know how you got your powers? Or even the extent of what you can do?

"I'm not discussing that with you. Cut the crap and get to the point."

"I want you. I want your soldier presence, I want your abilities, I want you to work with me."

White-Cell had seen the contemplation in Sau's eyes, he knew he'd crack anytime soon.

"If I'm so valuable to you, and you want me on your side, why are you taking your wrath out on innocent civilians?"

"Because, I needed to get your attention. Also, you're the hero, I am not."

"So you're offering me to join you, right? For what?" He thought about revealing what he did to his parents. Or even about the fact he has the only electrical component in the Pais. White-Cell decided vague honesty was the best choice.

"I want your powers."

"Man that's more delusional than when you said you could take over the world." Anger rose in White-Cell as he knew this would be harder than expected.

"You wipe the dirt with my generous offer? Huh, you got balls kid. Is that your final answer?" Sau nodded. "Well, these people's blood is on your hands." He pointed at the ceiling and shot down the lights from the launchers in his hand. Sau jumped and pushed everyone out the way of the falling lights. Once making sure everyone was safe, he went to the register area and saw that White-Cell had disappeared.

"He ran out of the store and flew towards the brand new construction site." A woman pointed to the direction. Sau jumped and followed to wherever White-Cell was going to invoke havoc.

A Hero

Sau finally had a clue where he was going. The high rise. He figured White-Cell had planned this all along. He saw the tall crane on the unfinished building in the distance. Running along buildings, Sau wasn't far off until he jumped on White-Cell's back steering him off course.

"Take it out on me! Don't hurt people who have nothing to do with it!"

"You had a choice but you spat in it." White Cell flew into a street light trying to knock Sau off, but he held his balance. Nearing the highrise, Sau noticed a reporting crew interviewing the workers in the hard hat area. If he saw it, then White-Cell saw it. Meaning it gave him more ways to get Sau distracted.

"Don't do it!" Sau yelled.

"Do it? Alright, if that's what you want." Before White-Cell could do anything, Sau started choking him from the back as White-Cell crashed onto a platform.

"You're sick man, all of this to prove a point? Do you not care about the life of these innocent people?!" They both locked eyes unaware of their surroundings. The workers around them feeling uneasy at the tense situation.

"Does it look like I give a shit about their lives?" White-Cell grabbed the metal poles he saw in the bin, then chucked them at Sau.

"Everybody clear out!" Sau yelled as he jumped from pole to pole sending them away from people. This gave White-Cell a few moments to head up the highrise as Sau made sure everyone was safe.

"Lightning Striker thank goodness. That maniac is trying to bring this building down." One of the workers yelled running towards him.

"Where is he?"

"I don't know, the guy is flying around throwing objects."

"Get your whole crew as low as you can. I got it." Sau ran around the whole level trying to find him. Turning the corner to head up a level, he was met with a punch to the face. He looked up to a hazy vision of White-Cell standing over him. His eyes showed a taunting aura.

"Most kids your age worry about money, cars, sex. You can have that all. Just. Say. Yes." Sau response was a quick punch to the nose. Following up with an uppercut that sent White-Cell through the wall.

"Take that as an answer." White-Cell got up and wiped the blood from his mouth.

"You'll be seeing me again." He threw a knife as it counted down the detonator. Sau ran towards him as the force of the explosion pushed them together. Punches connecting, they both fell down into a dirt mound. Sau got up to see him flying away. Before he could do anything, the crane was tipping over the ledge.

"Oh please just stay in place." He said aloud. Gravity got the best of it as the cran started falling. From the direction, it was heading towards the construction workers running away. Sau ran out the highrise and seared through the air. Throwing himself at the crane, he collided with it as it broke his fall. Dusting himself off, the crowd that had formed around him started to clap. He looked at the distance he forced himself out and was slightly amazed.

"Ladies and Gentlemen he's done it again. The superhero of Hawaii. Lightning Striker had just saved the lives of multiple men today." The news anchor said with her microphone into the mic. Alternating between him and the camera, she went closer to him as he wiped dirt from his eyes. "How does it feel to save lives again from that madman?" He'd seen a lot of haole reporters on tv due to him being a hero now. However, he knows that he's never seen this anchorwoman before.

"Uh, I'm just glad no one was hurt." Before she could ask any more questions, Sau took off in a flash. "That wasn't a news lady." He thought to himself.

"So any success with him joining?" Szcar asked.

"No. he's a stupid idiot. But that's alright. I declare war on Lightning Striker."

"How did you know it was him at first?"

"I never forget a face that's embedded into my mind. But we have to take him down. If he won't join me," there was a knock at the door. Szcar opened it to find two women and a seeker bodyguard. They walked into the smelly condo and looked around.

"Hello Alberta. Who's this?" Szcar questioned.

"This is Lilia. She works at a store and had an encounter with Lightning Striker."

"Oh yeah?" White-Cell stood up. "What happened?"

"W-well." She started to stutter. "A guy tried to rob me, then Lightning Striker comes in, and completely thrashes the guy."

"Tell him what you told me Lilia." Alberta pushed on.

"Well the robber shot the ceiling light and electricity sparks landed on Lightning Striker. When it made contact with him, he got more powerful. And even electrocuted the guy while his bare skin was touching him." Lilia stopped shaking.

"Well thank you Lilia for that." White-Cell smiled. Thinking to himself that he got the best gift in the world. "Now, how will you be rewarded? Ten thousand dollars?" He snapped his fingers at Szcar to get the money.

"No." She said abruptly. "I want to be a seeker."

"That's a painful process that only the tough come out of. Why?" This made him more interested.

"From what My cousin Alberta tells me, the power, the money, the corruption. I was made to be a seeker." She looked at Alberta who pointed her finger at the briefcase full of money and floated it to her.

"No guarantee you'll survive the dosage. Your mind though, it's sadistic isn't it? That's what we need." "I want to try." Lilia smiled and tilted her head to the side.

"Very well." White-Cell clapped his hands. "Lay down on the table. Szcar fetch me the needles. And Lilia, brace for the pain." White-Cell grabbed the needles and injected the point into the serum. He turned and saw Lilia closing her eyes while she's on her back. Shaking his head, feeling a knowledge of her dying within a couple of minutes.

"I'm ready." She said tense. He smiled and injected the Pais in her arm. A heavy dosage, an ounce more than what was put into Sau. The only difference is, he is the only one in the world that has the electrical form in him. Thirty seconds went by with no symptoms. "My skin feels cold. It's getting colder. It's, it's." Lilia shrieked as the serum flooded her veins. Her nerves kept making her shake as her skin got colder. The short spasms she started having became more violent as the seconds passed on.

"It's killing her!" Alberta yelled and tried to go to her but the seekers held her back. White-Cell smiled and shook his head as Lilia froze. Everyone's eyes widened in shock at what they were seeing. A layer of what looked like Diamonds covered her and hardened. Slowly after, her skin turned to normal and she opened her eyes.

"That felt good." She stood up. A sinister smile on her face. "Let's go get Lightning Striker."

A Realization

"You should think about it, you can't be a hero forever. At least a high school degree, come on man." Raymundo followed Sau all over the house trying to persuade.

"School isn't for everyone. Like you said, the consequence falls on me." Sau sat down watching the news.

"Man you're growing up too fast." He sighed. "But yet, I'm not you."

"Listen brother, I promise to re-think school." He flicked away from a commercial. "Anyways, man how can a villain get so messed up like White-Cell? How can any person do damage and endanger the lives of strangers with not a care in the world?"

"It's one of three things. He has had traumatic events in his early life, he lost someone close to him, or the worst of all, something very important was taken from him that he needed it."

"Why is that the worst of all?"

"Because he'll stop at nothing to get it. He won't care if some innocents die. So the question is, what does he want from you?"

"That's the thing, he asked me to join his team. I added it up to some world domination stunt."

"Highly doubt that, why would he choose Hawaii of all places? Second, that can't be the case because for a villain to want someone as a partner for that, he has to know what you can do. That must be the reason, a villain of his caliber wouldn't want just any scrub."

"So what're you saying? That I am above average?" Sau's childlike demeanor annoyed Ray.

"I'm saying, we have to find out what his true motive is. There has to be something, something that makes him tick." Raymundo stopped talking as he noticed Sau seemed to be preoccupied by his own thoughts. "What's going in your head bro?"

"That lightning strike, from that day at the football field. Before, I definitely knew I was different from the rest of the kids around me. It's just ever since that day, my powers seemed unreal to me."

"It mutated into something stronger most likely."

"Well, what are we going to do?"

"Lay low and stay put for a while."

"No Ray, I'm not hiding from him. I am a hero and I won't let this freak terrorize me or leave me in fear."

Ray smiled at Sau's sudden bravery. "Why're you looking at me like that?"

"Because little bro, you remind me so much of our mother. Our father may have been the bruiser, but our mother had a spirit like yours. I think a part of her lives through you." Ray moved from the computer and laid down on the couch while Sau was deep in thought.

"Yeah, maybe. Tell me something new about mom. Like on the daily, what was she like?" Sau rubbed his fingers through his head while his heart throbbed. "I miss her, and I never met her." Raymundo sighed and rubbed his eyes.

"She would always cook when there was an event. Birthdays, anniversaries, sports games."

"Sports games? I thought you didn't play sports until high school."

"No man, our dad played for the islanders. The developmental football league that folded two years ago." Sau was looking at Ray as if he found out they won the lottery. "Yeah man, it's true. That's probably where you got your football talent from. Dad met mom in college at Hawaii-Manoa, he was a crazy defensive lineman from the old film we used to have. And mom, she was his biggest fan. A true college romance."

"That's amazing. Did he get any chances to play in the NFL?" Ray smiled then shook his head.

"He was the best defensive lineman on the team, but the team wasn't really that good his final year. In fact, they were downright terrible. And that hurt his draft stock. After his pro-day, he sighed to San Francisco. Then missed the season cause he blew out his shoulder in training camp."

"Ouch." Sau sucked in his teeth. "It was really rough back then so I can only imagine how hard they were going."

"Yeah, and around that time, mom found out she was pregnant with me." Raymundo said as he flipped on the television. "Dad came back to the island, healed up, but for some reason, he never went back."

"Did you ever ask him why?"

"Sure did, a couple months before he died. We were watching the sunrise, you were playing a few feet away. He told me that it was fun playing football, but he only did that because it paid for him to go to college. To get away from his home life. He found his dream, to start a family. And he died trying to protect his dream, which was a success."

"That's a lot about dad, tell me more about mom." Ray gulped and shook his head.

"Not now, the pain of remembering her is still raw."

"At least you have memories of her." Sau shot back as that silenced Ray. The awkward silence lasted until Sau got up and went to his room. Ray wished he could go to his younger brother, but he knew that he was in the wrong.

Real Life

The heavy wind that blew against Sau's windows had awoken him again. In the early hours of the morning, thoughts already started racing through his head. Right about now, he'd still be asleep until his alarm went off for school. He sat up knowing he wouldn't go back to sleep right now, but to make use of this time.

Stepping outside of his house, he looked at the dark sky starting to brighten as the sunrise was on its way up. He observed his familiar suburban neighborhood, drastically different from how they grew up in the countryside.

"Couldn't sleep either huh?" Raymundo came to his side and sat down. "Yeah, you were always an early bird. About last night, Sau I have been around mom. I remember her last day here on earth. We both were there when we lost our father, but I also carry the pain of losing a mother." Sau now started understanding where Raymundo was coming from.

"I see why you don't want to talk about her all of the time, but can you see the reason why I do want to though?" Raymundo nodded. "Alright, so how about we meet somewhere in the middle. You tell me whenever you are ready, but you have to tell me everything you remember. Deal?" The brothers now looked at each other with a new found understanding.

"I can agree to that, sounds like a plan." They both looked up at the sky, a feeling of nostalgia washed over them. Remembering how their father used to watch the sunrise with them.

"Ray," they both still looked at the brightening sky as he acknowledged Sau. "It was always three of us. Our dad was the king, and we were his princes. Now, it's just us two. We can't lose each other, we are all we got bro."

"I know, damn Sau. You're only sixteen and having to go through shit. Always remember, you're stronger than you know. Just don't lose control." Ray's last statement had struck Sau differently for some reason. *Just don't lose control.*

"I won't brother. I don't know what everyday will look like, but I am ready for whatever comes our way."

One Step Ahead

"What are our orders?" Lilia asked, entering the lair's screening room.

"Orders? Oh yeah, I order you to stay back and manage my files." White-Cell rubbed his fading gray air as Alberta scoffed.

"You have other seekers on the job patrolling all day and night. We're seekers too, why not trust us? Why not let us help?"

"For your information, my seekers are more advanced and trained than you two. You both are fairly new, and very valuable. Until you fully know the extent of your powers, the dangerous missions aren't for you."

"What exactly is your goal here? The kid is not going to join you obviously. So what now?" Lilia crossed her arms waiting for an explanation.

"We may have a loophole, Szcar went back to our lab reports sixteen years ago. Found a chemical that can substitute for the electrical component we used in the boy."

"So let's say Szcar gets his hands on it, what happens then?"

"I can inject it into myself. I already have the Pais in my bloodstream. Add that to me, I'll be able to match Lightning Striker." White-Cell smiled to himself thinking of a glorious defeat before Alberta chimed in.

"When you had the sample sixteen years ago, why didn't you just inject it into yourself then?" He now faced the two and sighed.

"It was too powerful, I thought it'd kill me. So I wanted to test it on a weak baby, if the baby died then oh well. I would've got my answer. You know what they say, hindsight is twenty twenty."

"Back to the chemical you've found. Where is it?"

"Mayor's office, that's where all confidential stuff is held, especially all substances in medical procedures. Highly guarded too, but you know, the seekers are always willing to take a life." There was a silence as White-Cell thought for a moment. "Stay around ladies, I'll have plans for you both soon.

City Love

Sau loved walking the streets of downtown Honolulu. The busy place is where he could think most. Whenever him and Ray looked at the sunrise, it meant new beginnings. Walking down the busy streets, Sau had more time to think about his life. Only sixteen, and life has hit him harder than most his age.

He now thought about the hero thing. Wondering if he bit off more than he could chew, especially when it came to White-Cell. They hadn't had a run-in in a few days, but he knew White-Cell was plotting. While he was thinking, Sau walked in a store filled with his former favorite pastime, comics.

"Hey young man, welcome to my store. First time here?" The haole man at the register greeted him.

"Yeah, first time in this store. I've always loved comics though."

"Favorite superhero?" Sau thought about it and smiled, deciding to sniff something out.

"The new hero on the island, Lightning Striker. I'm pretty sure you know about him." Sau wanted to hear an opinion of himself, seeing what a civilian really thinks.

"Well, to be honest, I'm not a fan of people doing cops work. However, these shit cops can't stop these bad guys nowadays. That Lightning Striker though, I like what he's been doing. So many people are pushing for his own comic." Sau smiled at that statement.

"Really? How's that possible?" Sau asked. The man bent down behind the register and pulled out a big poster. Sau's eyes went wide at the poster of him in his costume. Pastels and watercolors bringing him out in his pose. "That's beautiful, people really love him, huh?"

"Yeah they do, little kids come in here and beg to know when a comic will come out. However, no one seems to be able to talk to him." Sau thought about that deeply. He saves people but has no personality in the media. It's not the most important thing he thought, but it wouldn't hurt.

"Thank you for your time, I was just window shopping. Have a nice day." He abruptly left the store as tears welled in his eyes. The doubt he felt earlier was completely erased. Sitting on a bench, he remembered a time where hope was little. To when he wasn't who he was now, back to when things seemed lost.

Flashback

Another day at school that blended in with the other days. As he sat down on the school bus, Sau looked out his window at the other middle school kids. Seeing them being picked up by their parents always rubbed him the wrong way. Jealous of not being able to have a mother, or a father anymore. Back on the big island, Sau remembered how his dad would walk home with him after school. Having multiple conversations to pass the time.

As the bus stopped in front of his house, the same feeling of dread washed over him. It happened everyday unless Ray was there, he hated being home with his foster people. He never called them his foster parents, they could never replace the ones he lost.

Heading inside the house, Sau hurried up the stairs to avoid any communication with them.

"Sau, come here Sau." He heard the "mother" call his name. He reluctantly went downstairs to the kitchen, knowing she'd be there. "How was school?" She asked while going through the mail.

"It was fine, just school."

"Well, right here in the mail, it says you're failing mathematics." Sau gulped as he never really paid attention in school. "Speak up boy." Mrs. Aweo ordered.

"I can get the grade up with no problem, I promise." Sau started to walk out of the kitchen until Mr. Aweo stepped in front of him.

"She wasn't done talking to you." He put his hands on Sau's shoulders and shoved him back. In a flash, electricity started sparking off of him as his anger rose. "You need to calm down." Mr. Aweo slightly held his hand out.

"That electricity is back, that is the devil in him. Manuel, I thought you beat it out of him!"

"I thought I did too, but that's just fine. I can stop this if he gets too rowdy." Sau noticed as Mr. Aweo started taking off his belt. Thinking fast, he snapped his fingers at him and him. Watching him twitch, Sau rushed and tackled his foster dad and started pummeling him while on top. A belt slash to the face sent Sau to the ground clutching his cheek. The rubber of the belt temporarily affected his powers.

"Honey, get up while he's down." She whipped Sau on the back to make sure he didn't have another chance to strike.

"This little hawaiian fuck, honey get me the knife." Mrs. Aweo went into the kitchen while Mr. Aweo stared Sau down. "Boy, I told you what would happen if you used that on me again right? Sad to tell Raymundo his little brother decided to run away."

"No, he didn't." Mr. Aweo turned to see Raymundo in front of him. In a split second Ray dropped him with a right hook to the jaw. As he dropped, she came back out with a knife, her eyes in dismay. "Raymundo, it's not what you think."

"Put the knife down." The staredown intensified when she clutched the knife tighter. Slowly, she started walking towards him. "Listen, I'll take my brother and just go." She didn't budge, but slowly kept walking. As she raised the knife, a flash of light blinded Ray as she went down. He looked and saw Sau with his hand out. Electricity flowing from his palm instead of fingers.

"Come on, we have to go."

"Go, where are we going?"

"Honolulu. The big city."

Brother In Arms

"So we're here, do you remember?" Raymundo asked Sau. They both stared at the Iolani Palace, in awe of remembering the past times.

"The parade two years ago, it was the best memory we had since Dad died at that time. That's so crazy.

You can live in a city for a while, and only go to the popular places a few times."

"When we first came here, I remember dragging you out the house. You moaned and groaned about how you wanted to just lay in bed, but that day was different for you. Hell, different for us."

"Why'd you bring me here Ray? It's a nice site but what's the reason?"

"It's a lesson, or motivation. We tend to be down in the gutters, then one thing happens for our moods, mindset or even life to change. I'm saying this Sau, with growing comes pain. You're not always going to be happy, you won't always be sad. It's life, gotta move with it." Sau now looked at Raymundo in a new light. Not only as a big brother, but now as a friend.

"I get what you're saying, I have some more stuff to learn for sure." While appreciating the moment, the sound of cars crashing into each other caught their attention.

"Get your suit on Sau." Looking around for the noise, it happened again, this time both being able to locate it. "It's just up the street, right by the intersection." Both hurried to the scene and stood in shock. Four men fighting off the police trying to get into the Mayor's building.

"Those are the seekers Ray. I've seen them before, they work for White-Cell."

"And whatever is in that building, it must be to kill for since they're throwing cars."

"Ray, stay back and only help innocents who are not in the crossfire. I'll handle these guys." Sau ran full speed at the one seeker who got prepared to throw another car at the officers in front of the building. Once in range, he pulled back his arm and let his fist connect with the seeker's face. Sending him down for the count.

"It's Lightning Striker!" One seeker yelled but was distracted by the gunshots fired from the police. The other two charged forward, Sau quickly evaded on and threw the other up into a light pole.

"I gotchu now bastard!" The other grabbed him from the back.

"Sucker." Sau smiled and deliberately jumped backwards into a car as hard as he could. "One more to go." Police stopped shooting as they saw Lightning Striker creeping behind the last seeker. As he turned, Sau jumped and did a flying knee to his chest.

"Goddamn!" The seeker trying to catch his breath on the ground. Sau grabbed him by the collar and pulled him forward.

"What is your purpose here? And what does White-Cell want?"

"Screw you, you fake ass punk bitch hero."

"Don't worry about that Striker," A policeman came up with a jar that had bars on the side of it. A small amount of greenish yellow liquid on the inside. "This supplement or whatever it is makes us think that this is the reason they were here. It was locked away deep in the mayor's office before it was snagged."

"I don't know what that is but we should keep it." Raymundo whispered in Sau's ear. He nodded and took the sample and studied it. Lost in the moment, he wasn't aware of his surroundings.

"Sau!" Looking up, the one seeker had a gun pointed directly at Sau. Freezing in the moment he closed his eyes knowing no matter how fast he was, he wouldn't be able to move. The seeker pulled the trigger before police tackled him. Opening his eyes, he saw his brother on the ground clutching his chest.

"Ray, no!" He jumped to the ground and held his brother. "No, no, please!" Ray could barely make out the words, but it was still audible.

"Don't wait for an ambulance. Put me on your back and rush there." Sau lifted him and sped to Honolulu city hospital. He lost his mother and father, he wasn't about to lose his only family left.

PLANNING

"Sir, I believe we have good news for you." White-Cell took off his shoes and stared at Szcar, making note that he didn't knock before entering. "Excuse my lack of manners."

"What is the good news?" Szcar stepped aside as the head seeker from the police standoff walked in.

"This better be good."

"White-Cell, we were on the mission trying to collect the component. Obviously we were fighting with cops and then came Lightning Striker."

"I see you came empty handed, if this leads to you not getting the samples, I promise to God I'll gut you where you stand." Szcar stood behind the seeker to make sure he couldn't run.

"So then what happened?" Szcar questioned

"We held off the cops for a while, Lightning Striker came and beat on us. Before most of the unit was whisked away to the jail, I had one more bullet. And shot his brother in the chest." White-Cell smiled enthusiastically and applauded.

"He has no family left. His brother must be dying as we speak. This is a major plus for not only me, but the seeker army."

"That is true White-Cell, however we don't have the component still. And I can guarantee that the mayor building is on lockdown now."

"Lightning Striker took off with the last of the rare samples."

"Where did he go?" White-Cell and Szcar got into the seekers face now.

"I heard his brother say Honolulu City Hospital."

"I'll have seekers raid the place right now."

"No!" White-Cell commanded. "We can work through this. Right now, he's probably doing everything he can to revive his brother. He'll be at the hospital some time. Alberta, Lilia!" The two came in a few seconds after and greeted him. "Want some work? I have a task for you to complete immediately." "What is it?" Alberta asked.

"I need you two to go to Honolulu City Hospital, look for Lightning Striker. He's most likely in the emergency room area."

"I doubt he's just in the hospital wearing his hero clothes, how can we spot him without his mask on?" "With these." Szcar gave Lilia and Alberta goggles that comfortably fit around their heads. "You can *see the electorpais when you turn those on. The fluid will show up as a series of green streaks in the person's body. Kind of like an x-ray."*

"Don't kill him though, you can beat him up of course but I just want two things. One, take the electorpais samples he has with him. Second, tell him if he wants to find out the truth of his parents, come see me atop of the Houla tower." Alberta and Lilia nodded at his orders. "Go, now!" With that, they both left.

"And what will we do?" The seeker asked.

"Me, Szcar, and a few others will be on our way to the Houla tower. You my friend, will be seeing your loved ones that passed." White-Cell lunged and sliced the seekers stomach open. "I don't care that you may have killed his brother. I should have gotten what I ordered for. Now you get to die in agony." White-Cell left the lair with Szcar as he mentally got ready for the battle ahead. It was time to reveal the truth.

SET UP

Sau sat anxiously in the waiting room not too long after bringing Raymundo to the hospital. His feelings were too intense as some electricity sparked off of him randomly. He remembered the story of his dad and brother waiting in the emergency room minutes before his mom passed.

"I can't lose Ray, I can never lose him. I'd have no one left." In a few moments, a nurse came out as Sau stood up and braced for the news. His heart was dancing on his tongue waiting to hear what she had to say.

"Mr. Titan, your brother's surgery to remove the bullet went well. He's up but a little dazed from the medicine." A big weight lifted off of Sau's shoulders. "However, I have to include something. The bullet was a big one, and damaged a lot of nerves. We had to call in other surgeons for an amputation, his right arm is dead." A terrible feeling washed over Sau, but he felt in that moment, as long as Ray was alive everything would be fine.

"Can I see him?" The doctor led Sau to the room they had Raymundo in, this being Sau's real first experience inside a hospital room. His eyes immediately darted to his brother's shoulder, seeing it all heavily bandaged up made it all the more real.

"You alright Sau?" Ray asked, still groggy.

"Am I alright? Man you're the one in the emergency room." They both shared a small laugh, happy to find light in this dark situation.

"I'll be right back, there seems to be something going on down on the first floor." The nurse said as she hurried out of the room. Sau thought something could've been serious but decided to put his brother first.

"Ray, you got shot bro. This is just crazy, and she told me the news. About what might happen to your arm." Tears welled in Ray's eyes as Sau mentioned that.

"No, I don't wanna lose my arm. There's got to be a way, there has to be."

"The nurse told me that the surgeons are on their way already, there's nothing we can do about that. I'm just glad that you're alive, and we're going to do whatever we can to keep you alive." Raymundo didn't like hearing that, but realized there was nothing he could do. "It'll be fine man, trust me. I'm here always." Sau moved closer to the bed and put the jar from the police on the desk.

"That's a serum of some sort, you can tell by how the fluid is rigid. It must be important enough for

White-Cell to fight Honolulu PD for it." Sau nodded as Ray studied it more. "That's interesting enough, Sau I've been thinking why White-Cell has been after you. Let's play devil's advocate. What if that stuff in your hand, is what was put in you as a child to save your life. Electorpais." Sau paused as he analyzed his brother's theory.

"It would make sense why he wanted me to join him so bad. Electorpais saved my life, and made me stronger. It's just a lot of what-ifs."

"That made you stronger eh? You almost died as a baby but that supplement kept you alive and here today." Ray studied the jar a little more closely, intense thoughts rummaging through his head.

"What're thinking Ray?" They both now looked at each other as if knowing what was going through their respective brains.

"Inject some of that into me, into my arm. If it worked for you, it'll work for me to keep my arm. Hell, wouldn't mind if it gave me powers too."

"I don't know. Ray this is a risk, I don't know how much was put into me. Yeah I can inject it into your arm, but are you willing to take a risk on your life?" He thought about it for a second before answering.

"Yes, do it Sau." Sau gulped and nodded. Grabbing a fresh needle from the drawer, he dipped it into the jar, filling the needle. Ray could see the nervousness in his brother's eyes and wanted to reassure him that everything would be fine. "No matter what Sau, this is my decision. Nothing is your fault, just remember that. Now hurry before the nurse comes back."

"Yeah, that *totally* made me feel better." Sau walked over to Raymundo's shoulder and removed a small part of the gauze. "Are you ready?" Raymundo nodded as Sau slowly put the needle to flesh. Once he was sure it penetrated, he pushed the liquid into Ray's body. "How is it feeling?"

"The shit is really cold man. It isn't painful, just cold. Damn, my arm feels so numb now." Panic started to rise in Sau, but he kept remembering that this was his brother's decision.

"You hear that?" Ray popped his head up towards the door. In the quiet seconds, they both heard the shrieks of nurses followed by the loud banging. "What do you think is happening?"

"I don't know, but I have to find out."

"Don't put on your gear, you just don't know what's out there yet." Sau took note and slowly peered out of the doorway. Almost half of the lights were out and the eerie feeling crept up on him. No nurse was in sight, almost as if time seemed to stand still.

"Ray, something isn't right…" Sau stopped as he saw his brother slumped over on the bed. A small amount of pus dripped out of his arm. "No, Ray!"

"Oh Lightning Striker! Where art thou Lightning Striker!" A mocking woman's voice echoed through the hall. Sau quickly geared up, and entered the hallway once again. This time, he was met with two women, both wearing goggles that flashed when they saw him.

"Who are you?" Sau charged up as he braced for a fight.

"Do it Alberta." The taller girl threw a metal object at Sau. As he dodged and rushed forward, he threw a bolt but was blinded by Lilia's diamond skin effect. In the blindness, Alberta delivered a blow to his stomach that sent him to his knees.

45

"Where are the samples?" Alberta kicked him in his jaw. Sau jumped and tackled her through the room in which his brother was supposed to be in. Looking up from the debris, the bed was empty. Before he could take note, Lilia hit him in the head with her diamond arm. In the daze, he jumped up and dashed to cover. His vision filled with stars, but he still knew this was a high pressure situation.

"Got the samples, what should we…" Her voice stopped as a wave of air knocked her out of the room. Alberta ran to her sister but was caught in the same gust that overpowered her. Sau slowly got up as he saw Raymundo, standing proud with a slight wind blowing around him.

"Dude, what did it do?" Sau asked in amazement.

"Seems like I can control air, but we have more important things to deal with right now." They stared down the two women that now stood to their feet. "They have the rest of the samples." Ray made note of it.

"So Lightning Striker and his brother, this is a sight. I can't believe White-Cell had a hard time taking you down." Ray tried to advance but Sau stopped him.

"What does White-Cell want from me, huh? Why does he keep messing with me, I never did anything to him." Sau pleaded as anger rose in him. "I'm starting to get annoyed by this, and I can't let you leave with those samples." Sau and Ray began to slowly walk forward.

"Should we tell them Lilia?" Alberta smiled and asked.

"Yes, right after this." Lilia used her diamond abilities to break the ground beneath Sau and Ray. As the attack caught them by surprise, the floor beneath them fell through as they did also. The fall hurt both brothers, but Sau was able to see above him the two girls. "Want to learn more about your parents? Come atop the Houla tower. That's where you'll find the samples and your answers. Better hurry heroes."

"Ugh, damn. What could she have meant by that?" Ray asked as he got out of the rubble.

"I don't know man. We just have to go and find out, especially about our parents. I'm starting to think your theory has more truth in it than we think. Something is up, and we're gonna find out." The brothers dusted the debris off of them and had a new objective in mind, to find out the truth.

Two Against All

"How does it feel having that stuff inside of you now?" Sau asked as they stood outside the Houla tower.

"I don't feel much different, but my abilities, being able to move air is so different, free almost. I think the thing that changed the most is my confidence. I can help you fight villains now man, just like we are about to now."

"Ray, what do you think they meant when they brought up our parents? I just don't understand."

"Don't worry, White-cell will make both of you understand." The brothers looked behind them and saw Szcar along with a few seekers. Before a move was made, Szcar grabbed Raymundo and blasted up the tower. The rest of the seekers surrounded Sau on the ground. Noticing he was outnumbered, he smirked at the fact they didn't know what was to come next.

"Don't worry brother, here I come. This won't take long at all."

Szcar dropped Raymundo on the top of the platform a little distance away from White-Cell. The air was more ominous as the rain and wind picked up.

"Big brother, nice of you to join me."

"What do you want? And what the hell do you know about our parents?!" White-Cell smiled as he began pacing back and forth.

"You weren't that old when he was born, but you were old enough to remember. Your mother, Tamina

Titan?" Raymundo now stood upright, knowing Szcar was right behind him, he kept his movements slow.

"What are you trying to get at?" That made White-Cell stop pacing, as he now looked him in his eyes.

"I was there when your mother took her last breath." Ray turned around and punched Szcar straight in the nose. Turning back around, he sent a gust of wind White-Cell's way as a warning. "Oh damn, an airbender? Somehow, you must've gotten this into you." He lifted up the jar of electorpais. "Feel powerful?" Before Ray could think of his next move, Lilia came and knocked him off his balance.

"Go Alberta!" He looked up and moved out of the way from her blow.

"Ladies handle him, I'll make use of this." They all watched as White-Cell gulped all the liquid down in the jar.

"That'll kill you!" Alberta screamed. Taking advantage of them being distracted, Ray threw wind power at Alberta and Lilia sending them backwards. Szcar's body came flying in front of Ray and hit White-Cell, taking them out for now. Looking to his right, Ray saw his little brother, looking like a heroic warrior. "Let's finish what we started." Sau and Ray agreed as they walked over to the girls. Lilia used her diamond arm and swung wildly at Ray while Alberta jumped and tried to get Sau with her gadgets. Ray being new to his powers couldn't gather his air attack quick enough, leading to him having to stay on defense. Sau threw a few bolts but Alberta's gear was able to counteract it and send them back. Both brothers have met their match in combat. Ray noticed Sau was having the same struggle as he was, being an aerial fighter wouldn't work in this situation.

"Sau, get back to back." The brothers went in position and clearly saw what was in front of them. Alberta and Lilia studied their respective opposition and advanced forward.

"Ray, gather up some wind, I got an idea." Ray breathed in then started to move the hectic air around them. "Pick a target!" Sau yelled as the wind got stronger and louder. Ray turned and directed the power towards Alberta. As Ray threw the wind, Sau threw an electric ball that mixed in and powered faster towards her. In the same second it hit her, Lilia used both Diamond arms to break the ground beneath them all. Falling through a few floors, they landed on a platform inside the tower. Its construction shows the bottom level in the works of renovation.

"Damn, my back is numb." Raymundo grunted as he slowly got to a sitting upright position. Sau rolled onto his stomach then rose to his knees. Both facing the same way, looking at what was left of the two girls.

"Ray, Alberta is singed." Sau whispered while looking at her limp body.

"That's not the only thing." He pointed at Lilias body, her midsection pierced as she had landed on half of a broken ladder. "I guess Karma came and collected early."

"You two stupid punk heroes!" The brothers quickly turned and dropped their jaws. White-Cell's body was morphed into that of a giant. Szcar on his side with a shotgun strapped to a rifle. "I lost two good lieutenants because of you. That's fine, this ends tonight."

"I'm surprised taking all of that supplement didn't kill you. Why're doing this White-Cell huh? And wha-" Sau dodged a bullet sent from Szcar. As he loaded another bullet, Sau sped up and sent an electric shot through his body. White-cell charged at Raymundo, hoping to throw his weight around to take him down.

"One trick pony." Ray jumped and threw a ball of air at White-Cell, slowing him down as he came with a kick to the head. He continued to take advantage of him being dazed and swept him from under his feet. "To be this powerful of a villain, you sure aren't smart." Ray taunted as he stood over him.

"Ha, that's outrageous. If I'm not the smart one, then how come you haven't found out that I'm the one who killed your dad?" Ray stepped back and froze in fear. It was at that moment, he knew he stared into the eyes of his father's killer. Those piercing blue eyes, the same ones that stared Sau and him down before he clawed into their father. "Cat got your tongue?"

"Y-you, killed my father. On that day, you took him from us." White-Cell hit Raymundo with an uppercut that sent him back on the platform. Trying to gather wind, Ray was cut in the back with a sharp blade.

"It burns, doesn't it? A cut up back is the least of your worries. You're gonna die, without ever getting revenge on the man who took away all of your loved ones." As White-Cell lifted his claw, an electric shock sent him back. Sau jumped down and tended to his brother.

"It's only a flesh wound, and he's down for now. Get up bro, we got this." Ray tried to get to his knees but the immense pain from the scratches left him to lay on his stomach.

"I can hardly move, he got me pretty good. You can take him though, one on one."

"Of course I can, I'm dinged up, but I can get him." Sau now looked down at White-Cell getting Szcar off of him, realizing this is one of their only one on one battles.

"Brother there is something you have to know, about what they meant about our Dad." Sau and Ray locked eyes now. Ray looked up as Sau looked down awaiting the answer. "I should've remembered all along. Those blue eyes, the ones that pierce your soul. Sau, that's the man who killed our father." A shiver that seemed to freeze Sau's spine crept up on him, almost paralyzing him in the process.

"So you finally figured it out, you dipshit?" White-Cell yelled across the platform. Fully to his feet, he began walking towards Sau. "Little Lightning Striker finally figured it out, would've been better if you found out on your own, but we're in the here and now. And now, your time is up. You worthless electric spark plug, I gave you the offer of a lifetime and you spat on it. To be what, a service dog everytime the weak needs your help? I'll do you a favor, and take you and your brother outta misery like I did your father."

"Sau, what's going through your mind? Sau!" Ray kept asking and shouting at him. The entire time White-Cell spoke, Sau was processing everything he had just learned. His father's killer was walking towards him. After all of these years, everything he had endured swirled through his head. In images, flashes, the experience almost overwhelming.

"I, will, avenge my father."

The Fight

Sau and White-Cell walked towards each other almost in a rhythmic cadence, eyes set on one goal, destroying each other. Tears streamed down Sau's mask as anger rose in White-Cell.

"All of my life, I knew this moment would come. I knew you were still out there." Sau whispered low to himself. His eyes now charged up with electricity, sparks flying off of him erratically. A short distance away, both stopped. No more words needing to be said at this moment. On this platform, it all ended here.

"Sau!" Ray had screamed with all his might, but it was no use. In a flash of a second, Sau tackled White-Cell then slammed him down. A wild array of punches being thrown between the two. Sau's electricity component and speed burned White-Cell's skin while White-Cell's strength and metal wore Sau down.

"I didn't care to kill your father, he just got in the way." White-Cell said amidst the struggle.

"Shut up!" Sau exclaimed as he lifted them both off the platform and landed on the lower floor. He threw bolts of electricity in a sporadic frenzie. Most of them hitting the structure instead of his main target. Soon, Sau made note of the building's structure. With all of the damage they had done, this tower could fall at any moment.

"I see you looking, the Houla tower's foundation can't handle your power. Look, it's beginning to crumble. I always win, *Lightning Striker.*" Sau looked him down, in the next moment he looked up for his brother Ray. Having to shield his eyes as the structure of the tower started to cave in. White-Cell now made himself visible, walking towards Sau again. "Time is running out, hero. Pick, either save yourself and your brother, or get revenge on your fathers killer. But see, since I don't need you anymore, once you let me get away again I'll get off scot free again." His sly smile made Sau's blood boil, but he had clarity. Clarity of the moment, as destruction poured down around him, he looked one more time into the eyes of White-Cell, his fathers killer.

"I never got to meet my mother, and you killed my father in front of my eyes. For years I struggled with the death of those two, but now, I will end this. Forever. The moment I look at the pacific ocean, and pray to Kanaloa, my past will not be the judge of me or my actions anymore." Sau garnered all of the energy he could muster, while White-Cell charged towards him.

"You will not defeat me boy, I made you! I gave you those powers, you belong to me!" Sau released all of the energy he had as the electricity exploded from his chest onto White-Cell. The attack left Sau drained as he sank to his knees. The place crumbling down even more, Sau looked across from him at White-Cell, his body burned to the core.

"Good job brother, good job." Raymundo said to himself from the upper platform. As he rolled over on his back, he knew in that moment, if he and Sau were to die from the tumbling building, he had made peace. Their father's killer is gone.

"Come on Ray." Raymundo looked to his side as Sau picked him up. "We are not dying here, we are not dying now. Use your air to fly, as I use my electricity as a boost."

"Sau, my back is numbing my body." Ray said before Sau abruptly picked him up.

"Ray, listen to me. You're the only family I have, I am not losing you too. Gather your strength, and we'll blast off. On three. One! Two! Three!" With all of their might, the brothers used their powers and blasted off the platform. With the Houla tower falling to complete destruction, Sau held onto Ray's arm as he flew through the air. Going to a place they haven't been to in years, a place that brings them peace.

Kaimana Beach

Sau looked over at his brother as they stared off into the water, the big bright pacific ocean on a grey cloudy morning. Their fight through the night against White-Cell couldn't bring them to sleep, but it got them to have peace.

"How do you feel, Sau?" Raymundo asked. Sau sighed before looking him in the eyes. The slight breeze adding the final calm moments.

"I feel fine. I feel like I'm just in the moment, living."

"Sau, you killed our fathers' killer. The first person you ever took life from, was the same one who took a life from us. You just feel fine?"

"Yeah, I mean, I don't feel guilty. I know for sure that I'm not a person to kill repeatedly, it's just like how you said, he took a life from us." They both now looked out into the ocean, tired, but a new feeling finally freedom.

"It's crazy to say it, but I think you would've been a momma's boy. You have her personality man, that's wild." Sau smiled and the return of his longing came. A longing to meet his mother, someone that he never knew. However, his longing wasn't mixed in with sadness, more of a sense of clarity.

"Yeah, I bet. How's your back?"

"Eh, it'll leave an ugly ass scar. But we are Titans, that is our name, and we are strong."

"Taking a page out of dad's book huh?" Sharing a laugh, the two heard laughter and the stir up of cars. The beach just now technically opened as visitors started setting up their places on the sand.

"Well Sau, we got some good ribeye back at the house. Taking out a villain leaves you with an appetite eh?" Raymundo started walking off as Sau looked back at the ocean. The clouds parted as the sun started to make the water shine. Taking a deep breath, he imagined breathing in his past. Exhaling, he opened his eyes, feeling as if at this moment, he knew his past couldn't hold him back anymore. He was free, getting rid of that black heart. His only intention was living for the moment.

A Plot

"Come on boss, this thing is ugly. You sure this is the same White-Cell from 84?"

"No more questions, Private. That's an order. Put him on the table." The men carefully put White-Cell on the metal table.

"Man, that Lightning Striker son of a bitch must've put a hurtin on this fellow." The men heard a knock at the door.

"At ease soldiers, it's a special guest." The captain opened the door as a man in a black cape came through. "Nice to have you here, Red-Cell."

"Where is he?" Without waiting for an answer, Red-Cell walked up to the table where he saw his brother lay. "Is he dead?"

"No, comatose. Don't worry, our former Navy medics will have him up and about in no time." The other soldiers backed up as Red-Cell walked around the table.

"Who's responsible for this? I want a name and location." His bloodshot eyes put fear into the captain.

"Lightning Striker. He always fights crime in Honolulu, but he can be anywhere. All we know is that he's in Hawaii." The captain grabbed a picture from the drawer. "This is the best picture we have on him." Red-Cell observed it and nodded. A clear colorized picture of the hero in full view.

"I can kill him right?"

"White-Cell wanted him for himself. But I don't think he'll mind if you take off a limb or two." Everyone laughed for a few seconds until Red-Cell's stare made everyone tense up again. "Lightning Striker." He held the picture in his hand. "I'll be seeing you soon."

All Is Good

The sun peeked through Raymundo's curtains as the early morning got started. Sau crept in his room, with a wicked smile on his face, he zapped Ray to wake him up.

"Damn, an alarm would've made more sense."

"That was an alarm, come on, you have powers now. It's time for you to know how to use them." Sau chuckled as he saw Ray trying to gather wind. "Don't make it so obvious, but can you hit lightning?" Just as Ray threw air, Sau dodged and ran down stairs. His brother quickly followed.

"What're you running for?" Ray and him stood in the living room, annoyance settling in as he saw Sau's amused face.

"I would love to play this game with you, however, it looks like we have a pending mission." Sau pointed to the TV as there was breaking news.

"Armed robbery in action at the military office downtown?" Ray questioned while looking at the news headline. Turning towards Sau, his little brother was already in his gear ready to go help. "You sure are taking this hero thing more seriously."

"Of course, I got my big brother to take care of. Gotta sharpen my skills, you can too for sure."

"Just remember, we always fight together. Like a team." They both nodded and shook hands. Racing outside of the house, Ray looked at Sau and realized there was something special in him. In that moment, he not only looked at Sau like a little brother. He now also looked at him as Lightning Striker, the hero of Hawaii.

Printed in the United States
by Baker & Taylor Publisher Services